★ THE ★
UNITED
STATES
PRESIDENTS

ANDREW JACKSON

Megan M. Gunderson

Checkerboard
Library

An Imprint of Abdo Publishing
abdobooks.com

ABDOBOOKS.COM

Published by Abdo Publishing, a division of ABDO, PO Box 398166, Minneapolis, Minnesota 55439. Copyright © 2021 by Abdo Consulting Group, Inc. International copyrights reserved in all countries. No part of this book may be reproduced in any form without written permission from the publisher. Checkerboard Library™ is a trademark and logo of Abdo Publishing.

Printed in the United States of America, North Mankato, Minnesota
052020
092020

THIS BOOK CONTAINS
RECYCLED MATERIALS

Design: Emily O'Malley, Kelly Doudna, Mighty Media, Inc.
Production: Mighty Media, Inc.
Editor: Liz Salzmann

Cover Photograph: Getty Images
Interior Photographs: Adam Jones/Flickr, p. 26; Albert de Bruijn/iStockphoto, p. 37; AP Images, pp. 17, 23, 36; Getty Images, pp. 5, 19; iStockphoto, p. 21; Library of Congress, pp. 7 (inauguration), 25, 28, 29, 31, 32, 33, 40; MPI/Getty Images, p. 13; National Archives, pp. 7, 27; North Wind Picture Archives, pp. 6, 11; North Wind Picture Archives/Alamy, p. 20; Pete Souza/Flickr, p. 44; Shutterstock Images, pp. 38, 39; Wikimedia Commons, pp. 6 (Rachel Jackson), 15, 40 (George Washington), 42

Library of Congress Control Number: 2019956427

Publisher's Cataloging-in-Publication Data
Names: Gunderson, Megan M., author.
Title: Andrew Jackson / by Megan M. Gunderson
Description: Minneapolis, Minnesota : Abdo Publishing, 2021 | Series: The United States presidents | Includes online resources and index.
Identifiers: ISBN 9781532193576 (lib. bdg.) | ISBN 9781098212216 (ebook)
Subjects: LCSH: Jackson, Andrew, 1767-1845--Juvenile literature. | Presidents--Biography--Juvenile literature. | Presidents--United States--History--Juvenile literature. | Legislators--United States --Biography--Juvenile literature. | Politics and government--Biography--Juvenile literature.
Classification: DDC 973.56092--dc23

★ CONTENTS ★

Andrew Jackson

Andrew Jackson was the seventh president of the United States. He was the first president to come from a poor family. Because of this, many people felt he represented the common man.

Growing up in South Carolina, Jackson had a difficult childhood. At age 13, he joined the **militia** to fight in the **American Revolution**. Jackson later established a successful law practice. Then, he became a leader in politics. During the **War of 1812**, Jackson proved he was a strong soldier. He became a national hero.

In 1828, Jackson was elected president. While president, he fought against the abuse of states' rights. Jackson also spoke out against the Bank of the United States.

Meanwhile, President Jackson and other leaders broke promises made to Native Americans. They forced many tribes to leave their land and move west.

Jackson was president for two terms. He then retired to his Tennessee plantation. From there, he continued to support his fellow **Democrats**. Jackson is remembered as a true representative of the people of the United States.

1767

On March 15, Andrew Jackson was born in the Waxhaw settlement in South Carolina.

1787

In North Carolina, Jackson became a lawyer.

1796

Jackson attended the convention that wrote the Tennessee state constitution. He was elected to the US House of Representatives.

1798

Jackson became a Tennessee Supreme Court judge.

1780

Jackson joined the militia and began fighting in the American Revolution.

1797

Jackson was elected to the US Senate.

1806

Jackson killed Charles Dickinson in a duel.

1791

Jackson married Rachel Donelson Robards.

1823

Jackson was reelected to the US Senate.

1828

Rachel Jackson died on December 22.

1814

During the War of 1812, Jackson won the Battle of Horseshoe Bend in Alabama.

1829

On March 4, Jackson became the seventh US president.

1832

Jackson vetoed a bill to renew the Bank of the United States. Jackson was reelected president.

★ ★   ★ ★   ★ ★   ★   ★ ★

1815

Jackson won the Battle of New Orleans and became a national hero.

1821

President James Monroe appointed Jackson military governor of Florida.

1830

Jackson signed the Indian Removal Act.

1845

On June 8, Andrew Jackson died.

" It is to be regretted that

the rich and powerful too often bend the acts of government

to their selfish purposes. "

ANDREW JACKSON

★ President Andrew Jackson is featured on the US $20 bill.

★ After Jackson's inauguration, a crowd caused trouble at the White House. They broke china, ruined furniture, and spilled punch. Jackson escaped the chaos and spent his first night as president in a hotel!

★ On January 30, 1835, Richard Lawrence attempted to assassinate President Jackson. This was the first time someone had tried to kill a US president. Luckily, both of Lawrence's guns misfired and Jackson was unhurt.

Frontier Childhood

On March 15, 1767, Andrew Jackson was born in the Waxhaw settlement in South Carolina. At this time, South Carolina was a British colony. Andrew's parents had moved there from Ireland in 1765.

Andrew's father was also named Andrew. He died before Andrew was born. Andrew's mother was Elizabeth Hutchinson Jackson. She worked as a housekeeper. Andrew had two older brothers, Hugh and Robert.

As a young boy, Andrew picked fights and had a bad temper. However, he also protected younger children. He taught them to shoot rifles, fish, race, and wrestle. Andrew learned to read books. Yet he was not very interested in school. Elizabeth wanted Andrew to become a minister. But he did not want this, either. Soon, the **American Revolution** interrupted Andrew's schooling.

FAST FACTS

BORN: March 15, 1767

WIFE: Rachel Donelson Robards (1767–1828)

CHILDREN: none

POLITICAL PARTY: Democrat

AGE AT INAUGURATION: 61

YEARS SERVED: 1829–1837

VICE PRESIDENTS: John C. Calhoun, Martin Van Buren

DIED: June 8, 1845, age 78

Andrew's birthplace was near the border of South Carolina and North Carolina.

Joining the Fight

The **American Revolution** reached the Waxhaw area in 1780. Andrew and his family helped tend the wounded. The same year, Andrew and Robert joined the **militia**. In August, they participated in the Battle of Hanging Rock in South Carolina.

In spring 1781, British soldiers captured Andrew, Robert, and other colonists. While captured, Andrew refused to clean a British officer's boots. For this, the officer slashed Andrew's arm and head with a sword. Robert also refused the officer. He was seriously injured as well.

The wounded boys were then forced to march to a prison. There, Andrew and Robert became sick with **smallpox**. Elizabeth secured their rescue. They were traded for British prisoners held in Waxhaw.

After the long trip back home, Robert died. Andrew was very sick, but his mother nursed him back to health. Then, she left to care for other sick prisoners. Elizabeth soon died of **cholera**. Andrew's brother Hugh had also died during the war.

The British officer's attack permanently
scarred Andrew's head and arm.

At 14, Andrew was alone. He tried living with relatives
and learning the saddle business. But he was not happy.
At 16, Andrew inherited money from his grandfather. He
quickly wasted the money. Then, Andrew briefly went back
to school. He even tried teaching, but he did not like it.

Tennessee Lawyer

In 1784, Jackson went to Salisbury, North Carolina. There, he studied law. He worked very hard. In 1787, Jackson became a lawyer.

The following year, Jackson moved west of the Appalachian Mountains to Nashville. This region of North Carolina would soon be the new state of Tennessee. At the time, this was as far west as the colonies reached. The land was wild, like Jackson!

In Nashville, Jackson began a successful law practice. He also met Rachel Donelson Robards. They fell in love and were married in 1791.

Five years later, Jackson bought a plantation near Nashville. He called it Hunter's Hill and built a house there. Mrs. Jackson developed Hunter's Hill into a successful plantation.

The Jacksons did not have any children of their own. However, they adopted Rachel's nephew in 1809. He took the name Andrew Jackson Jr. They also raised other nephews, including Andrew Jackson Donelson.

Rachel Jackson

A New Politician

In 1795, Jackson was elected as a delegate to the Tennessee **Constitutional** Convention. This event was held the next year. At the convention, Jackson and the other delegates wrote the Tennessee state constitution.

Then, Jackson was elected to the US House of Representatives. He was Tennessee's first representative. Jackson refused reelection. So, he left Congress on March 4, 1797.

Jackson then returned home. However, he was elected to the US Senate at the end of the year. He resigned his seat in 1798. That year, Jackson became a Tennessee **Supreme Court** judge.

After six years, Jackson went back to work on his plantation. That year, he sold Hunter's Hill and purchased a new plantation. The Hermitage was also near Nashville.

Meanwhile, Jackson became known for fighting in **duels**. A lawyer named Charles Dickinson insulted Mrs. Jackson. So in 1806, Jackson challenged him to a duel. Dickinson was killed, and Jackson was shot near the heart. The bullet stayed in his chest for the rest of his life.

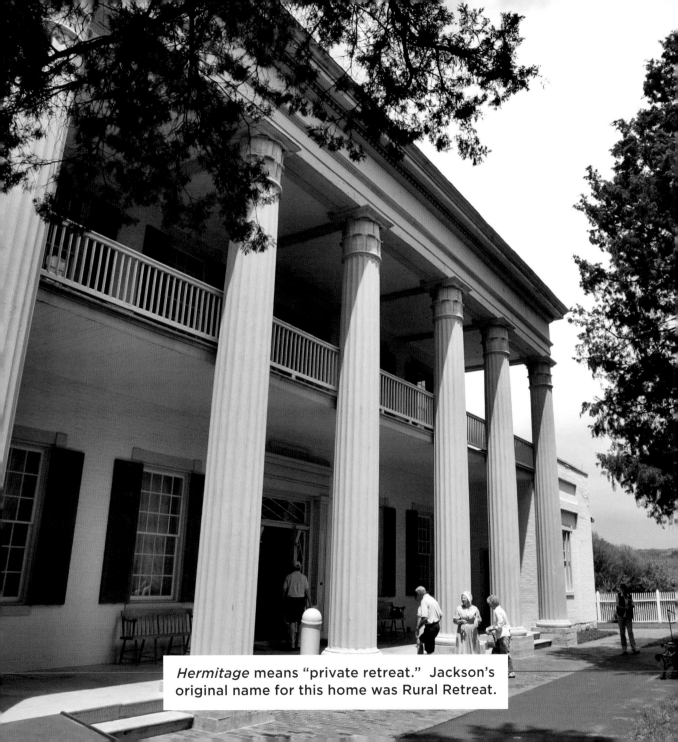

Hermitage means "private retreat." Jackson's original name for this home was Rural Retreat.

The War of 1812

When the **War of 1812** began, Jackson joined the fight. He had been elected major general of the Tennessee **militia** in 1802. Now, Jackson led his men in many big battles in the South.

The men soon called their tough leader "Old Hickory." This is because hickory is one of the hardest, toughest kinds of wood.

At the time, many Native Americans were angry with the US government. American settlers were taking over their land. So, they fought with Great Britain against the United States.

Jackson's militia faced Creek Native Americans in several battles in 1813 and 1814. Finally, on March 27, 1814, Jackson and the Tennessee militia won an important victory. They defeated Creeks at the Battle of Horseshoe Bend in Alabama.

This victory earned Jackson a promotion. He became a major general in the US Army. Now, he was in charge of soldiers in Tennessee, Louisiana, and the Mississippi Territory.

After the Battle of Horseshoe Bend, Creek leaders were forced to sign a treaty giving the United States about 23 million acres (9.3 million ha) of land. This land was in Georgia and Alabama.

War Hero

The **War of 1812** continued. So after his promotion, Jackson was sent to defend New Orleans, Louisiana. There, he added to his group of soldiers. Free African Americans and even pirates joined him! Other new volunteers were Tennessee and Kentucky riflemen and planters.

On January 8, 1815, Jackson triumphed again in the Battle of New Orleans. Nearly 2,000 British soldiers were hurt or killed. Fewer than one hundred of Jackson's troops were hurt or killed. This great victory made Jackson a war hero.

Afterward, he went home to the Hermitage. In December 1817, President James Monroe gave Jackson new orders. Jackson went to defend settlers in

The Battle of New Orleans

Today, a statue of Jackson stands in
Jackson Square in New Orleans, Louisiana.

Georgia along its border with Spanish Florida. Seminole
Native Americans were crossing the border to attack the
settlers. This conflict became known as the First Seminole
War. In 1818, Jackson marched into Florida. He captured

Pensacola and Saint Marks. In 1821, the United States gained control of Florida. President Monroe appointed Jackson military governor of the territory.

At the end of the year, Jackson resigned. Then in 1823, the Tennessee legislature reelected Jackson to the US Senate. He served two years before resigning.

Meanwhile, Jackson decided to run for president. In the 1824 election, he received 99 electoral votes. John Quincy Adams received 84 and William H. Crawford received 41. Henry Clay won 37. No candidate had won a majority. So, the US House of Representatives had to choose the winner.

Clay threw his support behind Adams, who won the election. Then, Adams appointed Clay **secretary of state**. Jackson felt Clay had supported Adams so they could both get into office.

This incident helped form the Jacksonian **Democracy** movement. Jackson and his supporters felt the voices of the people had not been heard. Jackson vowed to fight for the American people.

Right away, Jackson started planning his next presidential campaign. In 1828, Jackson won! He received 178 electoral votes, while President Adams won just 83. John C. Calhoun was elected Jackson's vice president.

Vice President John C. Calhoun

President Jackson

Shortly after the election, tragedy struck Jackson's life. On December 22, 1828, Rachel Jackson died. Jackson was very sad. He blamed his wife's death on his political opponents. During the campaign, they had spread terrible rumors about Mrs. Jackson.

On March 4, 1829, Jackson was **inaugurated** as the seventh US president. People came to the White House to celebrate their hero. The crowds were so large Jackson had to escape through a side door!

Jackson's niece Emily Donelson acted as White House hostess. Andrew Jackson Jr.'s wife, Sarah Yorke Jackson, also served as hostess.

As president, Jackson often sought advice from outside his **cabinet**. This small group of friends included politicians and newspaper editors. They became known as the Kitchen Cabinet.

While Jackson was president, relations with Native Americans were challenging. Cherokee, Seminole, and other Native American tribes were losing more and more land.

Jackson's inauguration was the first to be held at the east entrance of the US Capitol.

In 1829, Georgia took over land that the United States had guaranteed to the Cherokee. The US **Supreme Court** ruled against Georgia's actions. However, Jackson did not enforce the ruling.

Instead, Jackson signed the Indian Removal Act of 1830. It stated that all Native Americans had to move west of the Mississippi River. Eight years later, 15,000 Cherokee were forced to move west. More than 4,000 of them died. This tragedy became known as the Trail of Tears.

Meanwhile, President Jackson and Vice President Calhoun disagreed about the **Tariff** of Abominations.

Today, there are historical sites along the Trail of Tears route.

It placed high taxes on foreign goods. President Adams had passed the tariff in 1828 to protect Northern businesses. Jackson supported it. But Calhoun felt it was unfair to the South. People in his home state of South Carolina were especially upset.

President Andrew Jackson

Final Years

President Jackson did **not** run for a third term. On March 4, 1837, Van Buren was **inaugurated** as the eighth US president. Jackson then retired to the Hermitage. He was 69 years old.

Jackson had been ill for many years. He had **tuberculosis** and had lost his sight in his right eye. In addition, Jackson still ached from old wounds.

Yet Jackson remained active. He watched over his plantation and received many visitors. Jackson also stayed active in the **Democratic** Party.

He supported Van Buren for reelection in 1840. In 1844, he supported Democrat James K. Polk for president.

Jackson's actions influenced politics for many years after his presidency.

Martin Van Buren was Jackson's secretary of state and then his vice president. From 1837 to 1841, Van Buren served as US president.

On June 8, 1845, Andrew Jackson died. He was buried at the Hermitage next to his wife, Rachel.

Jackson is remembered as a tough leader. He stood up for the common man. Jackson fought for what he felt was best for the American people.

BRANCHES OF GOVERNMENT

The US government is divided into three branches. They are the executive, legislative, and judicial branches. This division is called a separation of powers. Each branch has some power over the others. This is called a system of checks and balances.

★ EXECUTIVE BRANCH

The executive branch enforces laws. It is made up of the president, the vice president, and the president's cabinet. The president represents the United States around the world. He or she oversees relations with other countries and signs treaties. The president signs bills into law and appoints officials and federal judges. He or she also leads the military and manages government workers.

★ LEGISLATIVE BRANCH

The legislative branch makes laws, maintains the military, and regulates trade. It also has the power to declare war. This branch consists of the Senate and the House of Representatives. Together, these two houses make up Congress. Each state has two senators. A state's population determines the number of representatives it has.

★ JUDICIAL BRANCH

The judicial branch interprets laws. It consists of district courts, courts of appeals, and the Supreme Court. District courts try cases. If a person disagrees with a trial's outcome, he or she may appeal. If a court of appeals supports the ruling, a person may appeal to the Supreme Court. The Supreme Court also makes sure that laws follow the US Constitution.

THE PRESIDENT ★

★ QUALIFICATIONS FOR OFFICE

To be president, a person must meet three requirements. A candidate must be at least 35 years old and a natural-born US citizen. He or she must also have lived in the United States for at least 14 years.

★ ELECTORAL COLLEGE

The US presidential election is an indirect election. Voters from each state choose electors to represent them in the Electoral College. The number of electors from each state is based on the state's population. Each elector has one electoral vote. Electors are pledged to cast their vote for the candidate who receives the highest number of popular votes in their state. A candidate must receive the majority of Electoral College votes to win.

★ TERM OF OFFICE

Each president may be elected to two four-year terms. Sometimes, a president may only be elected once. This happens if he or she served more than two years of the previous president's term.

The presidential election is held on the Tuesday after the first Monday in November. The president is sworn in on January 20 of the following year. At that time, he or she takes the oath of office:

> *I do solemnly swear (or affirm) that I will faithfully execute the office of President of the United States, and will to the best of my ability, preserve, protect and defend the Constitution of the United States.*

LINE OF SUCCESSION

The Presidential Succession Act of 1947 defines who becomes president if the president cannot serve. The vice president is first in the line of succession. Next are the Speaker of the House and the President Pro Tempore of the Senate. If none of these individuals is able to serve, the office falls to the president's cabinet members. They would take office in the order in which each department was created:

Secretary of State

Secretary of the Treasury

Secretary of Defense

Attorney General

Secretary of the Interior

Secretary of Agriculture

Secretary of Commerce

Secretary of Labor

Secretary of Health and Human Services

Secretary of Housing and Urban Development

Secretary of Transportation

Secretary of Energy

Secretary of Education

Secretary of Veterans Affairs

Secretary of Homeland Security

While in office, the president receives a salary of $400,000 each year. He or she lives in the White House and has 24-hour Secret Service protection.

The president may travel on a Boeing 747 jet called Air Force One. The airplane can accommodate 76 passengers. It has kitchens, a dining room, sleeping areas, and a conference room. It also has fully equipped offices with the latest communications systems. Air Force One can fly halfway around the world before needing to refuel. It can even refuel in flight!

Air Force One

If the president wishes to travel by car, he or she uses Cadillac One. It has been modified with heavy armor and communications systems. The president takes

Cadillac One

Cadillac One along when visiting other countries if secure transportation will be needed.

The president also travels on a helicopter called Marine One. Like the presidential car, Marine One accompanies the president when traveling abroad if necessary.

Sometimes, the president needs to get away and relax with family and friends. Camp David is the official presidential retreat. It is located in the cool, wooded mountains of Maryland. The US Navy maintains the retreat, and the US Marine Corps keeps it secure. The camp offers swimming, tennis, golf, and hiking.

When the president leaves office, he or she receives lifetime Secret Service protection. He or she also receives a yearly pension of $207,800 and funding for office space, supplies, and staff.

Marine One

George Washington

Abraham Lincoln

Theodore Roosevelt

	PRESIDENT	PARTY	TOOK OFFICE
1	George Washington	None	April 30, 1789
2	John Adams	Federalist	March 4, 1797
3	Thomas Jefferson	Democratic-Republican	March 4, 1801
4	James Madison	Democratic-Republican	March 4, 1809
5	James Monroe	Democratic-Republican	March 4, 1817
6	John Quincy Adams	Democratic-Republican	March 4, 1825
7	Andrew Jackson	Democrat	March 4, 1829
8	Martin Van Buren	Democrat	March 4, 1837
9	William H. Harrison	Whig	March 4, 1841
10	John Tyler	Whig	April 6, 1841
11	James K. Polk	Democrat	March 4, 1845
12	Zachary Taylor	Whig	March 5, 1849
13	Millard Fillmore	Whig	July 10, 1850
14	Franklin Pierce	Democrat	March 4, 1853
15	James Buchanan	Democrat	March 4, 1857
16	Abraham Lincoln	Republican	March 4, 1861
17	Andrew Johnson	Democrat	April 15, 1865
18	Ulysses S. Grant	Republican	March 4, 1869
19	Rutherford B. Hayes	Republican	March 3, 1877

THEIR TERMS ★

LEFT OFFICE	TERMS SERVED	VICE PRESIDENT
March 4, 1797	Two	John Adams
March 4, 1801	One	Thomas Jefferson
March 4, 1809	Two	Aaron Burr, George Clinton
March 4, 1817	Two	George Clinton, Elbridge Gerry
March 4, 1825	Two	Daniel D. Tompkins
March 4, 1829	One	John C. Calhoun
March 4, 1837	Two	John C. Calhoun, Martin Van Buren
March 4, 1841	One	Richard M. Johnson
April 4, 1841	Died During First Term	John Tyler
March 4, 1845	Completed Harrison's Term	Office Vacant
March 4, 1849	One	George M. Dallas
July 9, 1850	Died During First Term	Millard Fillmore
March 4, 1853	Completed Taylor's Term	Office Vacant
March 4, 1857	One	William R.D. King
March 4, 1861	One	John C. Breckinridge
April 15, 1865	Served One Term, Died During Second Term	Hannibal Hamlin, Andrew Johnson
March 4, 1869	Completed Lincoln's Second Term	Office Vacant
March 4, 1877	Two	Schuyler Colfax, Henry Wilson
March 4, 1881	One	William A. Wheeler

Franklin D. Roosevelt

John F. Kennedy

Ronald Reagan

	PRESIDENT	PARTY	TOOK OFFICE
20	James A. Garfield	Republican	March 4, 1881
21	Chester Arthur	Republican	September 20, 1881
22	Grover Cleveland	Democrat	March 4, 1885
23	Benjamin Harrison	Republican	March 4, 1889
24	Grover Cleveland	Democrat	March 4, 1893
25	William McKinley	Republican	March 4, 1897
26	Theodore Roosevelt	Republican	September 14, 1901
27	William Taft	Republican	March 4, 1909
28	Woodrow Wilson	Democrat	March 4, 1913
29	Warren G. Harding	Republican	March 4, 1921
30	Calvin Coolidge	Republican	August 3, 1923
31	Herbert Hoover	Republican	March 4, 1929
32	Franklin D. Roosevelt	Democrat	March 4, 1933
33	Harry S. Truman	Democrat	April 12, 1945
34	Dwight D. Eisenhower	Republican	January 20, 1953
35	John F. Kennedy	Democrat	January 20, 1961

LEFT OFFICE	TERMS SERVED	VICE PRESIDENT
September 19, 1881	Died During First Term	Chester Arthur
March 4, 1885	Completed Garfield's Term	Office Vacant
March 4, 1889	One	Thomas A. Hendricks
March 4, 1893	One	Levi P. Morton
March 4, 1897	One	Adlai E. Stevenson
September 14, 1901	Served One Term, Died During Second Term	Garret A. Hobart, Theodore Roosevelt
March 4, 1909	Completed McKinley's Second Term, Served One Term	Office Vacant, Charles Fairbanks
March 4, 1913	One	James S. Sherman
March 4, 1921	Two	Thomas R. Marshall
August 2, 1923	Died During First Term	Calvin Coolidge
March 4, 1929	Completed Harding's Term, Served One Term	Office Vacant, Charles Dawes
March 4, 1933	One	Charles Curtis
April 12, 1945	Served Three Terms, Died During Fourth Term	John Nance Garner, Henry A. Wallace, Harry S. Truman
January 20, 1953	Completed Roosevelt's Fourth Term, Served One Term	Office Vacant, Alben Barkley
January 20, 1961	Two	Richard Nixon
November 22, 1963	Died During First Term	Lyndon B. Johnson

Barack Obama

	PRESIDENT	PARTY	TOOK OFFICE
36	Lyndon B. Johnson	Democrat	November 22, 1963
37	Richard Nixon	Republican	January 20, 1969
38	Gerald Ford	Republican	August 9, 1974
39	Jimmy Carter	Democrat	January 20, 1977
40	Ronald Reagan	Republican	January 20, 1981
41	George H.W. Bush	Republican	January 20, 1989
42	Bill Clinton	Democrat	January 20, 1993
43	George W. Bush	Republican	January 20, 2001
44	Barack Obama	Democrat	January 20, 2009
45	Donald Trump	Republican	January 20, 2017

★ PRESIDENTS MATH GAME ★

Have fun with this presidents math game! First, study the list above and memorize each president's name and number. Then, use math to figure out which president completes each equation below.

1. Andrew Jackson + Chester Arthur = ?

2. Warren G. Harding + Andrew Jackson = ?

3. Benjamin Harrison − Andrew Jackson = ?

Answers: 1. Woodrow Wilson (7 + 21 = 28)
2. Lyndon B. Johnson (29 + 7 = 36)
3. Abraham Lincoln (23 − 7 = 16)

LEFT OFFICE	TERMS SERVED	VICE PRESIDENT
January 20, 1969	Completed Kennedy's Term, Served One Term	Office Vacant, Hubert H. Humphrey
August 9, 1974	Completed First Term, Resigned During Second Term	Spiro T. Agnew, Gerald Ford
January 20, 1977	Completed Nixon's Second Term	Nelson A. Rockefeller
January 20, 1981	One	Walter Mondale
January 20, 1989	Two	George H.W. Bush
January 20, 1993	One	Dan Quayle
January 20, 2001	Two	Al Gore
January 20, 2009	Two	Dick Cheney
January 20, 2017	Two	Joe Biden
		Mike Pence

★ WRITE TO THE PRESIDENT ★

You may write to the president at:

The White House
1600 Pennsylvania Avenue NW
Washington, DC 20500

You may email the president at:

www.whitehouse.gov/contact

★ GLOSSARY ★

American Revolution—from 1775 to 1783. A war for independence between Great Britain and its North American colonies. The colonists won and created the United States of America.

cabinet—a group of advisers chosen by the president to lead government departments.

censure (SEHNT-shuhr)—to officially express disapproval.

cholera—a disease of the intestines that includes severe diarrhea.

constitution—the laws that govern a country or a state.

democracy—a governmental system in which individuals or elected representatives vote on how to run their country.

Democrat—a member of the Democratic political party. When Andrew Jackson was president, Democrats supported farmers and landowners.

duel—a formal fight between two people using weapons in the presence of witnesses.

inaugurate (ih-NAW-gyuh-rayt)—to swear into a political office.

militia (muh-LIH-shuh)—a group of citizens trained for war or emergencies.

secede—to break away from a group.

secretary of state—a member of the president's cabinet who handles relations with other countries.

smallpox—a contagious disease marked by a fever and blisters on the skin. The blisters often leave permanent scars shaped like little pits.

Supreme Court—the highest, most powerful court of a nation or a state.

tariff—the taxes a government puts on imported or exported goods.

tuberculosis—a disease that affects the lungs.

unconstitutional—something that goes against the laws of a constitution.

veto—the right of one member of a decision-making group to stop an action by the group. In the US government, the president can veto bills passed by Congress. But Congress can override the president's veto if two-thirds of its members vote to do so.

War of 1812—from 1812 to 1815. A war fought between the United States and Great Britain over shipping rights and the capture of US soldiers.

ONLINE RESOURCES

To learn more about Andrew Jackson, please visit **abdobooklinks.com** or scan this QR code. These links are routinely monitored and updated to provide the most current information available.

★ INDEX ★